baby animal tales

Goodnight, Little Penguin

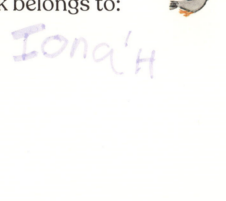

This book belongs to:

Iona'H

MAGIC CAT PUBLISHING

Once upon a bedtime,
there was a little penguin.

He lived far, far away at the bottom of
the world, in a land of ice and snow.

Little Penguin kept cosy and warm,
sitting safely on his daddy's feet,
snuggled up in his soft, warm feathers.

Time passed, and Little Penguin grew and grew.

Soon, he was big enough to waddle around
on the snow all by himself.

Pitter, patter he went.

Pitter, patter!

More time passed and Little Penguin
had grown some more. Now he could waddle
and hop and flap his tiny wings.

Hop, hop, hop he went.

Flap, flap, flap!

"What a clever little penguin you are!"
said his mummy who had come
back from the sea with fish for them all to eat.

Little Penguin grew and grew and grew until he
was too big to sit on his daddy's feet any more.

"You are such a hungry little penguin,"
said his mummy and daddy. "Now we
both need to go to the sea to catch fish."

"Can I come?" asked Little Penguin.

"The journey will be too long and cold for a little penguin like you," said his mummy. "You will have to stay here with the penguin nursery."

Little Penguin didn't like this idea one little bit.

Suddenly, a line of baby penguins
appeared, trudging across the snow.

"Quick, catch up!" called the last in
the line. "Your mummy and daddy will
be back before you know it."

But Little Penguin didn't want to join in.

He stood all on his own at the edge of
the snowfield and soon he was very cold
and miserable indeed.

Brrrr! shivered Little Penguin.

"Won't you come and have fun with us?"
asked the baby penguin.

"I didn't want to go to nursery,"
Little Penguin said, stamping his little feet.

"And I don't want to play -
I just want to go home!"

Stomp, stomp, stomp!

"Alright," said the baby penguin sadly.
"But come and find us if a storm comes,"
she said, looking up at the sky.

"You won't be safe
here on your own."

It wasn't long before the wind
began to howl.

Hooo
woooo!

Hooo
woooo!

Snowflakes started to swirl.

Soon, Little Penguin couldn't see
where he was going.

Poor Little Penguin was
cold and wet and frightened!

Then, through the blizzard, he heard someone
calling him. It was the penguin from before.

"Come with me," she chirped.
"You must be getting cold out
here all by yourself."

This time, Little Penguin followed
and soon he was snuggled up with all the
other baby penguins, safe and warm.

The storm passed
and the sun came out again.

"Time to play!" cried the baby penguins,
and this time Little Penguin joined in.

First, they made
footprints in the snow.

Pitter patter!

Hop! Flap! Jump!

Then, they played hopping and flapping and sliding along the ice on their tummies.

Wheeeeee!

Little Penguin had so much fun that he didn't
even notice his mummy and daddy arrive.

"Time to go home," said Mummy. "You must be
tired after all that playing. Would you like to come
to penguin nursery again tomorrow?"

"Yes please," said Little Penguin with a yawn.
And that's just what he did.

Goodnight, Little Penguin.

MAGIC CAT PUBLISHING

Baby Animal Tales © 2020 Magic Cat Publishing Ltd
Text © 2020 Amanda Wood
Photographic illustrations © 2020 Bec Winnel
Photographic images used under license from Shutterstock.com
Illustrations © 2020 Vikki Chu
First Published in 2020 by Magic Cat Publishing Ltd
The Milking Parlour, Old Dungate Farm, Plaistow Road, Dunsfold, Surrey GU8 4PJ, UK

A catalogue record for this book is available from the British Library.

ISBN 978-1-9161805-9-8

The illustrations were created digitally
Set in Above the Sky, Recoleta and Cabin

Published by Rachel Williams and Jenny Broom
Designed by Nicola Price

Manufactured in China, TLF0620

9 8 7 6 5 4 3 2 1

FSC
www.fsc.org

MIX
Paper from
responsible sources
FSC® C104723